Secrets in the Hills of Turat

Jeruto Chepkwony

Published by BookPublisingWorld in 2021

ISBN 978-1-8381944-5-1

BookPublishingWorld
is an imprint of
Dolman Scott Ltd
www.dolmanscott.com

Contents

An early morning surprise!

K'pkeu the warrior found it difficult to wake up that morning. He had had a dream in his sleep — obviously an important dream — but why couldn't he recall what he had dreamt? He was slowly stepping out of his bed when he heard a knock on his door. He frowned and shook his head. *Argh, too early*, he thought. It was only seven in the morning.

He opened the door, and there were his nephews Yegon, Jemu and Jesir!

"Uncle, uncle!" they yelled. "Look up from the backyard to the hills."

They walked ahead of him, letting him follow. Curious, K'pkeu hurried after them. What could be happening?

"Hey!" K'pkeu called out, trying to keep up the pace. "Wait for me!"

At the backyard, he looked up. From where he stood, he could see the Turat hills clearly. He could not believe what he saw!

Turat was the home of their ancestral spirits. It was believed that when the elders died, their spirits went to live in the hills, and remained there for eternity. The belief was that these spirits would be watching over the community and guarding them against the bad spirits and from danger.

The house on the hill

K'pkeu now craned his neck, unable to believe what he was staring at. In the middle of the hills stood the most beautiful house he had ever seen. It was then that he recalled his dream of the previous night. In his sleep, he had a vision of a similar house.

Turat village had only 500 residents, and was a peaceful place. It was located next to Turat hills, which were named after the village. The hills were full of grass, flowers, herbs, and all sizes of acacia trees. The plants in the hills formed a beautiful, flat pattern, like a bed. Viewed against the patches of granite rocks, the hills looked even more beautiful.

From the top of the hills, you could see the entire village down the valley and beyond. If you looked carefully, you could see Koong'asis, a valley bordering Turat village. You could also see a foreign country known to the villagers as Misiri.

The village was named Turat in memory of their ancestors, who were buried in the hills. Twice a year, the villagers went up the hills to celebrate the New Year harvest known as Tumto.

Over the years, the villagers had come to love and respect the hills. But this day was different. All around, a man, woman or child could be seen gazing at the hills. Just where had that house emerged from? K'pkeu ran his eyes from the villagers to his nephews. Everyone was speechless.

Looking for answers

Perhaps the house appeared in the middle of the night, like a strange mushroom sprouting from the earth. K'pkeu studied the house; its walls were the colour of white spring granite. As the sun rose, the roof glistened, sending a blinding beam of light into the village. K'pkeu and his nephews looked away, for a moment blinded by the bright light.

Just then, K'pkeu turned to his nephews. "Let's go to your mother's house," he said. "I am also going to see Lorem, the Chief. I must find out what is going on."

"Can we come?" Yegon, Jemu and Jesir asked, obviously begging.

K'pkeu shook his head. "No. No. but I will tell you everything I hear from Lorem."

The four began walking down the road. As they did, they ran into K'pkeu's sister, Jerotich.

"What is happening?" she asked. She looked a little worried.

"I don't know, sis, but I am on my way to Chief Lorem's place. Where is Lomket, my in-law?"

"He has already gone to the Chief's place," Jerotich replied.

At that, K'pkeu left them. As he began walking away, he turned to his nephews and said, "I will be back as soon as possible. Now listen to your mother, children."

Enemies from the south

He made his way along the paths of the beautiful village. Members of Turat all knew each other. Every man, woman and child here was related to everyone else in the village. They were somewhat like a large family. This is why it was taboo to marry within the same village.

Men brought wives from outside the village; the women were married off to men in far-away villages. Throughout, there was plenty of food and people had enough to eat. There was a lot of livestock and plenty of grass for the livestock. The village lacked nothing.

At night, K'pkeu and other Turat warriors guarded the village from the southern enemy tribe, whose men stole their livestock under the cover of darkness. That southern tribe was the only one from which Turat village could not marry. The southern tribesmen were hated and feared by the Turat people.

When they sneaked in to steal from Turat, they also took with them food and killed anybody who resisted — including women and children! The thought of losing his own tribesmen or women to the enemy tribe sent a shiver down K'pkeu's spine.

As he walked on, K'pkeu recalled that, 10 years before, his sister Jerotich married Lomket from Kasige village. At the time, Kasige was affected by drought. Besides, all their livestock had been stolen and they had been left without enough food.

Even more waiting!

Because they had many problems, Lomket's family was allowed to come and live in Turat village. They and K'pkeu became friends. Jerotich and Lomket married and had three children: two girls (Jemu and Jesir) and one boy called Yegon.

Many times, the children were noisy and made trouble, but when Lomket and K'pkeu told them warrior stories, the children paid attention.

As he walked on, K'pkeu thought fondly of his nephews. Oh, he loved them. He arrived at the Chief's place at the time when the early afternoon sun was high up in the sky and was scorching hot. Already, Lomket was there, sitting with the other warriors.

"Is there any news?" K'pkeu asked.

He was told that there was no word about the house on the hill.

They waited for an hour before Chief Lorem arrived. With him was the village Orkoyoon. As the leaders approached, everyone stood up in honour, then sat back down.

Then the Chief began: "So there is a house on the hill and nobody knows how it came to be there, huh?"

The men at the Chief's place exchanged blank stares.

The Chief continued: "The Orkoyoon suggests that we wait. This could all be a sign from our ancestors. Perhaps our ancestors are trying to tell us something important."

Reports of an alien woman

Everyone was puzzled. What did all this mean? Was this the end of the world? Or was it a special sign from the ancestors?

At that point, the Orkoyoon spoke: "I also do not understand what is happening," he muttered. "We must wait. In the meantime, we will convene a meeting by the Council of Elders."

The Council of Elders decided to heed Orkoyoon's advice: there was little else to do but wait. Perhaps the strange house would go away the same way it had appeared. But what if it did not go away? What if something dangerous followed? The Chief had a clear warning for everyone: no matter what happened, no one was allowed to go up the hills.

While everyone waited, a daring team of hunters decided to take matters into their own hands. They sneaked off and went up the hill. Soon, they brought back the news that the owner of the house was a woman. They had seen her walking to the cornfield close to the house, but they were not able to speak to her.

Who could she be? Where had she come from? What powers had she to build a house on the very hills where their ancestors were resting? And how did she manage to build this house overnight?

The villagers arrived at a frightening conclusion: the woman had to be a witch. Or perhaps she was one of the long-gone aunts of the tribe.

What did she want? What had brought her back?

Warriors are sent out

As days went by, the weather slowly changed. At first, it began to rain. Then there was more rain, and even more rain. It rained for a week. When the rain stopped, the people of Turat village came together again for an emergency meeting. They were worried.

"My people," Chief Lorem began, "I will keep this short. As you all know, strange things have been happening. I am talking about the house on the hills and the woman whom the hunters saw. You have seen with your own eyes that it has rained continuously for a week now. Nobody has left the village."

The Chief paused to run his eyes through the villagers, then he said: "Now that the rain has stopped, I suggest we select a few men to go up the hill and bring the woman down so we may know what her business is." At that, the gathering of villagers began to whisper.

"At last! At last!" everyone agreed.

"Alright then!" the Chief said with a voice full of authority. "Let the hunters — K'pkeu, Komen, Jeremia, and chemos — go up the hills. You will leave early in the morning for the house on the hill."

After some murmuring among the villagers, the Chief added: "We all have had a long day. Let's all go back to our homes and get some rest. There will be some extra warrior-hunters available in case they are needed as a backup."

Facing the strange woman

Slowly, the crowd dispersed and everyone went home. Although they were still afraid, they were somewhat reassured: at least there would be some answers the following day. Still, they worried about what tomorrow might bring. Were their children safe? Would the end be painful?

That night, the guards kept watch in shifts, talking in low tones. From the huts around Turat, the voices of the villagers could be heard. As the night wore on and the wind blew in a soft breeze, the fire dimmed and the village went silent.

K'pkeu didn't sleep at all. He was preoccupied with thoughts about the house on the hills. In his life, he had seen many strange happenings. But that house and the woman bothered him.

Early the next day, he took some water and picked his spear. Then he hurried to the meeting point. All warriors convened at the foot of the Turat hills at dawn.

The anxiety in the eyes of the men told K'pkeu that they were scared. None of them had slept a wink. After the usual exchange of greetings, none of the men uttered another word. Their thoughts were on the strange house and the strange woman. What awaited them?

At K'pkeu's signal, they began the climb. The path wound around trees and meandered along rocky patches of the hills. After about an hour of ascending, they approached the house. Now they knew real fear.

Disappointment

K'pkeu looked down at the village; it all looked quiet and peaceful. Finally, they drew close to the house and, hesitating, the men all knocked at the door. They waited! No one answered. Carefully, they pushed open the door. The place was empty. In one corner was a fireplace. Here, there was the smell of burning meat.

"She's not here," K'pkeu murmured. "Let's check the cornfield."

They stepped out and did a quick search. There was no sign of the woman. The warriors sat under an acacia tree close to the cornfield and discussed what their next move would be.

"I think it's best to go back," K'pkeu said. "There isn't enough water, the morning sun is now hot, and the woman is nowhere to be found."

Komen, Jeremia and chemos nodded in agreement, and the warriors rose and returned to the village.

"She wasn't there," they reported.

Lorem the Chief said, "No worries: In five days, we have to go up the hill for the annual harvest celebration." He turned to the warriors: "In the meantime, keep watching for new developments on the strange woman."

The following day, and the one after, appeared to drag on forever. Time appeared to have slowed down. Within the five days, nothing happened. Throughout, Jemu, Yegon and Jesir remained quiet.

Fearful times

On the day of the new harvest celebrations, Chief Lorem called the people together and said, "My people, do not be afraid. It is time for celebration. The four hunters will go up the hill to clear the way. And you know they are the best warriors Turat has ever had. Let us enjoy!"

The people agreed. Soon, they broke out in song and dance as they made their way up the hills.

It was a beautiful day. At that hour, the sun was shining. Children ran about. Everyone was happy again. When they arrived on the hilltop, the villagers busied themselves preparing the tented camps. They erected wooden benches in the middle of the hill square. Although no-one mentioned the strange house or its inhabitant, fears about the woman remained.

When the villagers were resting, Chief Lorem and the elders convened a meeting. "Listen!" the Chief began, "I want this mystery solved, and I want it solved now!"

He turned to the four hunters and addressed them: "You, you, you and you." He was pointing at K'pkeu, Komen, Jeremia, and chemos. "Join me at the upper hill. We must re-enter the house." Then the Chief pointed at the rest of the gathering: "Make sure the harvest preparations proceed." Then, to the hunters, he gasped: "Alright, let's go!"

On the way, the Chief asked many questions: "What did the woman look like? Was she old? Did she talk to you?"

ε 333

Turat village beware!

"We couldn't see her clearly," Jeremia answered. "But from the little we saw, she had long, black hair and she wore a golden necklace. That's all we could see."

"Right?" the Chief asked, and looked at the other three.

"Yes, it's true," they said together.

After a short climb, the team arrived at the house. From up close, the house was even more beautiful. It was a square house; the roof was made of what looked like glass.

Usually, village houses were brownish-red, but this house was white. It reflected the sun, which made it difficult to look directly at it.

Using his stick, the Chief knocked at the door. Then, quite aloud, he announced: "I am Chief Lorem from Turat village. Open the door!" They waited for a response. No one answered.

"Open this door at once!" he said to Jeremiah.

Jeremiah and Komen pushed in the door and it opened with a faint creaking sound. Everyone stepped inside.

They were stunned. The woman sat in the middle of the room!

"Come, sit down," she said calmly.

They men exchanged curious stares. Why didn't she open the door when they had knocked?

The unnamed spy

As they stepped further in and sat, Jeremia observed the woman. She reminded him of his mother. She had a kind face and a soft voice.

The woman spoke again: "My name is Tula. I came to warn you. There is a traitor in your village. But you must find out who he is. He has been leaking important information to your enemy."

Chief Lorem now spoke: "But that is impossible! All our people are loyal. Our Council of Elders and our warriors are secretive and discreet about important matters. I have the finest warriors in the whole County."

Tula spoke again: "This person has been giving away information for more than a year now. You must be careful. The enemy knows all your moves. I can only guide you. Your ancestors sent me; they continue to look out for Turat from the sky. But you must be willing to follow my advice. You need to find this person. Be modest; he might bring great harm to Turat."

Chief Lorem and the hunters exchanged stares. A traitor among them? There was a spy in their midst? But they knew everyone in Turat!

K'pkeu was busy thinking. The woman had said: *He has been leaking important information to your enemy…The enemy knows all your moves.*

If that was true, this enemy had access to important information. But only the Council of Elders had access to that kind of information.

K'pkeu continued to think. *Could it be the treasure keeper? The blacksmith? One of the warriors?*

K'pkeu's new troubles

Suddenly, the Chief spoke: "I think we all know what to do. Everyone has to keep an eye on everyone else! Trust nobody?"

K'pkeu was busy thinking: *My father, my uncles and my friends are in the Council of Elders. What if the traitor is someone close to me?*

He turned to the men and said: "Fellow warriors, we have always trusted each other. But now we must act as spies; we must be suspicious of each other."

As much as K'pkeu wanted the traitor caught, he could not stomach the idea of keeping an eye on the people close to him. Without warning, he stood and rushed out. As he ran, the other men wondered: was K'pkeu the spy?

K'pkeu ran and ran. He stopped at the bank of Embobut River. He was thinking of returning to the men when he heard his friend, Jeremia, calling: "K'pkeu, stop! Stop! What's the matter with you?"

When Jeremia reached the river bank, he asked, "What is going on? How can you storm out like that? You are making the rest of us suspicious. You must come back with me. We need to find the traitor among us."

K'pkeu looked at his friend and shook his head. "Believe me, I am not the spy, Jeremia. I could never betray my people. I left because I was sick of the idea that it could be one of us?"

K'pkeu and Jeremia turned and slowly walked back in the direction of the mysterious house.

Prisoners of Turat

At the house, they were confronted by the Chief, whose remaining two warriors stood at the ready. One of the men furiously pointed his spear at K'pkeu and Jeremia. Without warning, the warrior lashed out at K'pkeu, hitting him on the side of his face with a *sitet* that was lined with poison.

The last thing K'pkeu heard, before he fell to the ground, was the angry voice of Chief Lorem.

The Chief was shouting: "Arrest them!"

Early the following day, K'pkeu stirred. He turned on his side and slowly sat up. The first thing he became aware of was the pain on the side of his head. He touched his head lightly. There was a wound just above his eye.

The spot was tender. It was also encrusted with blood.

"You are awake, K'pkeu?" Jeremia asked from his place on the floor.

"Where are we?" K'pkeu asked.

"We are prisoners."

"Prisoners? Why? What crime have we committed?"

Just then, K'pkeu remembered the Chief's words: *Arrest them!*

Slowly, his mind cleared. He recalled that he had run out of the mysterious house. Jeremia had persuaded him that they should return to the house on the hill. So they were now prisoners.

"Where are we?" K'pkeu asked.

Jerotich's surprising visit

"They tied us up and dragged us down Turat hill. Then they threw us in this cabin. It is a cell within the Chief's camp."

K'pkeu looked around. Although the wooden cabin was dark, a ray of light filtered in through a gap between the planks on the wall. There was just enough light to notice that the cabin was mostly empty.

K'pkeu tried to stand but the pain in his head was too much. He sat back on the earthen floor as he moaned. Then he turned to Jeremia: "What

are we going to do? What are they going to do with us?"

In the half darkness, Jeremia shrugged his shoulders.

"I don't know, K'pkeu. I guess all we can do is wait. We must keep telling them the truth — that we are innocent." Jeremia asked, "But why did you run? What was the matter with you?"

"At the time, I was not thinking," K'pkeu replied.

K'pkeu rose to his feet. He shook the door but it was locked from the outside. What were they going to do?

At dusk, just before darkness set in, there were noises outside the door. When the door was pushed in, two people entered. One was a warrior. He carried a spear. The other was Jerotich, K'pkeu's sister.

As Jerotich stepped further in, the warrior shouted at her: "You have only a moment to talk to your brother."

At that, the warrior stepped out. He locked the door from outside.

The shocking news

"Here!" Jerotich said to K'pkeu.

She handed over a bundle of leaves. K'pkeu took the bundle and unfolded it. Inside were several pieces of boiled meat. He picked one piece and began eating.

"Have a piece, Jeremia," K'pkeu said.

Jeremia accepted the bundle and selected a piece of meat. When he began eating, he carefully placed the bundle between himself and K'pkeu.

"I am not even sure I can eat," K'pkeu said, placing his half-eaten piece of meat back on the leaves. "My head hurts."

Jeremia swallowed the final portion of his piece of meat. He turned to Jerotich, asking: "So, any word on the traitor? What is going on outside there? Do people still think that I am the traitor?"

Jerotich remained silent for a moment. When she began to talk, she quickly closed her mouth. Then she began to cry.

K'pkeu sat straight up.

"What is it, sister?"

"It is not my fault," Jerotich whimpered. "I think Lomket is involved."

"Lomket? My bother-in-law? Your husband? But how? How do you know that? How can you even say such a thing?"

Just then, there were heavy footsteps outside, and Jerotich knew that the warrior had come to escort her out.

Prison break!

As the door was unlocked and the warrior stepped in, Jerotich looked with pity at her brother.

"Lomket wants a second wife. He is courting a girl from the south."

The warrior stood at the door. He gestured at Jerotich to step out of the cell.

As K'pkeu's sister made for the door, she turned to her brother.

"Do you remember the game we used to play as children, when I was naughty and father locked you in the house?"

K'pkeu stared at Jerotich. As she was led away, she gave him a look that told him she cared deeply about him.

When the warrior had led her away and locked back the door, Jeremia looked at K'pkeu.

"Lomket is the traitor? He can betray us after all the help we have accorded him?"

"No! My sister is wrong on this," K'pkeu said. "I trust my brotherin-law. I trust him with my life."

Jeremia picked another piece of meat from the leaves, then he said, "Your sister is Lomket's wife. She would not make such an accusation unless she is sure about this."

In the dead of the night, when everyone had gone to sleep, K'pkeu and Jeremia thought they heard a noise just outside the door of their cell.

Whispering in the night

From outside, someone shook the door but it would not yield. There was some struggling, perhaps even some cutting. Then the door was slowly pushed in.

"Shhh…" Jerotch said. She was holding a finger to her lips. She wanted them to remain silent. K'pkeu and Jeremia got the message. They were not to make a sound. Jerotich was breaking them out of prison!

Together, the three tiptoed out. Just outside, a warrior who sat against the cell had fallen asleep. In the distance, another warrior was busy stoking the fire. He did not hear the three tiptoe away from the Chief's camp.

Soon, the three were hurrying beyond Turat village. Jerotich led them towards Misiri, a foreign country that bordered Turat. They walked for a long time, until they approached Koong'asis valley.

"We must stop here," Jerotich suddenly said.

"By now the warriors must have discovered that we broke out of the cell," Jeremia said. "If they catch us, they will surely kill us."

"Jerotich added, "But if I let you remain prisoners, you two would be hanged because everyone in Turat now believes you are the traitors. And there is more: Turat village is about to be attacked. If I didn't break you out, all of us in Turat would either be killed, or we would be prisoners."

"What are talking about, sister?" K'pkeu asked. "You are scaring us. Please tell us what you mean."

The traitor is known

"I will show you. But do not make a sound."

With Jerotich leading, the three tiptoed through the bushes until they were close to the valley. Just then, Jerotich went down on her belly and crawled. K'pkeu and Jeremia also went down on their stomachs and crawled after her. What could be the matter?

Jerotich parted a bush and pointed to a section below, within Koong'asis valley. K'pkeu's head still throbbed with pain, but he could not believe what he saw. Five warriors sat around a fireplace inside the valley.

As one of the warriors stoked the fire, a large flame from the burning wood lit up a huge section of the valley. It was then that K'pkeu saw it.

Behind the warriors there was a large stockpile of spears, bows and arrows.

"They are preparing for battle!" K'pkeu said.

"Yes, the southern village is getting ready for battle," Jerotich added.

"They are preparing to attack Turat!"

"How would you know that, sister?" K'pkeu asked.

Just then, a man emerged from behind the pile of weapons. It was Lomket, Jerotich's husband. When he began to address the warriors, K'pkeu and Jeremia listened. At first, Lomket only whipered. Then, after he had explained something, he now spoke more loudly.

Lomket was saying: "We attack in two days. I want Turat defeated. Once we defeat Turat, the southerners will take everything."

A plan to save Turat

Lomket continued: "We will take their cows, goats, sheep, and their wives too. We will kill their men. I will marry the daughter of the southern Chief. I might even become the new chief of Turat."

As he listened, Jeremia cried out: "Oh *Asis*! Oh *Asis*, please help us. If we don't do something, our people are doomed. But what can we do?"

"I will show you," Jerotich said. "But you must remain in the bushes here. Keep an eye on the warriors. I must return to Turat."

Early the following morning, Jerotich entered the Chief's camp. By then, Lorem the Chief was furious. The escape of K'peu and Jeremia had been discovered. Already, scores of warriors were combing the area, looking for the two convicts.

Jerotich saw Chief Lorem just outside the wooden cell. She rushed to him and fell to her knees at his feet.

She cried to him, saying, "Punish me, good Chief, for I have offended Turat. I have offended our ancestors."

"What is going on, Jerotich?" the Chief asked.

"Our village, Turat, is about to be attacked. I broke K'pkeu and Jeremia out of prison?"

"You did what?"

Quickly, Chief Lorem summoned a warrior. "Place her under arrest now!"

Turat is free!

As the warrior approached, Jerotich shouted: "My husband, Lomket, has conspired with our enemies from the south. They are preparing for battle. They attack in two days. I took K'pkeu and Jeremia to Koong'asis. They are watching over the enemy. They are innocent. Believe me, good Chief!"

As the warrior began to arrest Jerotich, the Chief said, "Wait!"

Within minutes, all the warriors of Turat were summoned. By nightfall, they surrounded Koong'asis and took control of the large supply of weapons. K'pkeu, now a free man, led the warriors. Jeremia helped him.

They searched everywhere but they could not find Lomket.

Under the leadership of Chief Lorem, the people of Turat village continued with their search for harmony with their hostile enemies. One day, perhaps, they would find Lomket and understand the reasons for his betrayal.